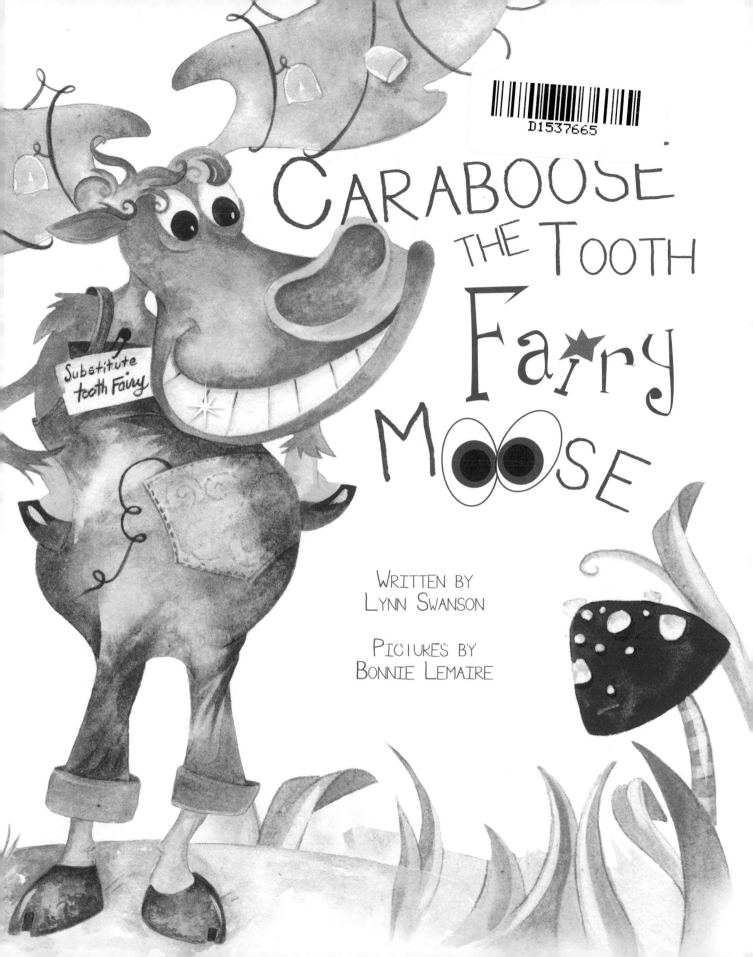

CARABOOSE THE TOOTH Fairy Moose

Substitute tooth Fairy

WRITTEN BY
LYNN SWANSON

PICTURES BY
BONNIE LEMAIRE

Available On:
CreateSpace.com\3686496
Amazon.com (ISBN 1466317337) or other retailers

TO LEARN ABOUT OTHER BOOKS BY LYNN SWANSON
including:
Summer Dance—fiction for ages 10-13
OR TO ARRANGE A BOOK READING OR SIGNING
GO TO:
www.lynnswansonbooks.com

USA copyright registration for "The Collected Works of Lynn Swanson": TXu 1-769-577
ISBN: 1466317337
ISBN 13: 9781466317338
Library of Congress Control Number: 2011916633
CreateSpace, North Charleston, South Carolina

Acknowledgment

Thank you to the Vermont Studio Center
for a generous scholarship and splendid space to be.

Dedication

This book is dedicated with joy to:

Karl, Katie, Boyd
and
To all children who wiggle their teeth

Do you have a loose tooth
or a space in your head
where your old tooth came out
or hangs loose by a thread?

Did you wiggle and jiggle
that tooth 'til it croaked,
let it float in a jar
'til it got over-soaked?

Did you tell all your friends
how it stuck on your toast
when you took a big bite
and they hollered "Gross!" ?

Then maybe you're ready
to give up your tooth
to fairies and magic
and me – Caraboose!

See, sometimes tooth fairies
go off to conventions
to trade magic potions
and other inventions.

They pack up their bags
and fly straight to Cancun
or Aruba or Brussels
or even the moon.

They leave me in charge
of old teeth for a week –
while they're on vacation
they want me to peek

through the window at you
while you snore in the night
to see if you put
your lost tooth away right.

4

They loan me their magic
their wands, all their loot
to trade for your beautiful
lost baby tooth.

They tell me to find you
asleep in your bed
to lift up the pillow
scrunched under your head

6

to see if you carefully
hid your old tooth
there where I'd find it,
not in a phone booth!

'Cuz some kids will wiggle
their tooth all day long
pretending they're reading
or humming a song

when really they're trying
to pop the last threads
to drop it some weird place
and I don't mean their beds!

They leave trails of old teeth
in wild bushes and thistles
in washers and dryers
in jars of green pickles.

How can I find them
in marbles and string
in fishbowls and earmuffs
and phones that don't ring?

How can I give your
lost tooth to the fairies
to dance around toadstools
or flowers or berries?

How can the fairies
exchange it for luck
if it's under your brother's
scratched-up hockey puck?

You have to believe
in the fairy tooth moose
while shaking and wiggling
your tooth 'til it's loose.

Then carry it home
in your pocket from school
keep it in there while
watching T.V. as a rule.

Smile big at your folks
when they put you to bed
let the empty space shine
in that place in your head

where your tooth used to sit
before it came out
where now there's a space
big enough for a trout!

Your folks will say:
"Ohmygosh! Where did it go?"
And you say with your eyes wide:
"I really don't know!"

12

Then remember I told you this
over and over:
Put it under your pillow
just up from your shoulder

not under the dresser
or next to the couch
or inside a tea cup
at grandmother's house.

13

When the tooth fairy tells me
to gather your teeth
she means you should leave them
for me on your sheet.

First
I'll do my great moose dance
while you're still asleep
quietly, gently
I won't make a peep.

Then
I'll put your white tooth
on my necklace so bright
with other kids' teeth
I've collected that night.

I'll go out the front door
and head straight for my house
in the trees near the toadstools
where good fairies crouch.

14

Your tooth will be safe
'til the fairies get back
carting their luggage
on fairy-car racks.

They're counting on me
to hand over the necklace
while they're having tea
at their fairy-tooth breakfast.

So don't be a wiggler
who drops off a tooth
in a jar of green pickles
or dusty phone booth.

Take it home in your pocket
and put it to bed
on top of your mattress
right next to your head.

I'll gallop through traffic
to pick up your tooth,
take it back to the fairies
who'll say: "Caraboose,

thank you for stringing
old teeth on our chains.
Please give them to us now
and give us the names

of the kids they belonged to
when they were brand-new
and we'll cook up a bucket
of magic-tooth brew."

They'll drop your tooth into
a big pot of goo
and magic will float
from the pot back to you.

20

And you'll be so happy!
You'll know your old tooth
has brought you good luck

thanks to

Caraboose Moose!